# THE CAPTURE

ERIKA WILDE

Copyright © Erika Wilde, October 2014

All rights reserved. No part of this book may be used or reproduced in any manner whatsoever without permission except in the case of brief quotations embodied in critical articles and reviews. This book is a work of fiction. Names, characters, places and incidents are either products of the author's imagination or used fictitiously. Any resemblance to actual events, locals, or persons, living or dead, is entirely coincidental. All rights reserved. No part of this publication can be reproduced or transmitted in any form or by any means, electronic or mechanical, without permission in writing from the Author.

# THE CAPTURE

There isn't much that Jillian Noble can resist when it comes to her sexy, gorgeous husband, Dean. She's become very independent in her daily life, but privately, behind closed doors, Jillian finds she loves submitting to her husband's more dominant, erotic demands.

When Dean surprises her with an Invitation to Eden and promises to fulfill one of her secret fantasies, she can't wait to find out what's in store. While on the mysterious island, she's auctioned off to a rogue pirate and imprisoned as his slave. What he commands of her is shocking, but there is no denying this dark, forbidden stranger, or the exquisite pleasure that comes with her ultimate surrender.

# CHAPTER 1

It was time to shake things up again. After six months of indulging in some of the hottest sex of his married life, Dean Noble was about to make one of his wife's secret fantasies a reality. With a click of his mouse, he sent off the final email that would approve all the plans and details he'd carefully orchestrated over the past few weeks and set into motion three days of seduction and ultimately, Jillian's surrender.

He leaned back in his office chair and smiled to himself, impressed with his own creativity. He'd never been one of those hearts and flowers kind of guys when it came

ERIKA WILDE

to romancing his wife, but since that day Jillian walked into his office and made it clear she wanted to elevate their sex life after twenty years of marriage, he'd found many ways to entice her mind and body—with erotic toys, leather restraints, and wicked demands.

Oh, and *pearls*, he thought with a private, lascivious grin. She'd especially loved what he'd done to her with that long strand of smooth, round beads.

Their physical intimacy had gone from routine and predictable to exciting and smoking hot. After suppressing his more dominate tendencies for fear of going too far and hurting Jillian in some way, she'd coaxed his darker desires to the surface, and welcomed and accepted the man who preferred to be in control in the bedroom. It hadn't taken him long to discover that his newly sexually adventurous wife liked things a little rough and dirty, with him in charge of her pleasure.

The level of passion in their marriage had escalated beyond anything they'd ever experienced together. Beyond the great sex, they

THE CAPTURE

were also learning to communicate and compromise—something he'd always found difficult to do because of his strong, alpha personality—and he had to admit that married life with Jillian, even after twenty years, was pretty damn good.

"What's with that smug look on your face?"

Dean glanced up as his Noble and Associates business partner and best friend, Brent "Mac" MacMillan strolled into the office then dropped his big, solid frame into one of the leather chairs in front of his desk. "I was just thinking about how much I love being a married man."

"Yeah, yeah, *I know*," Mac said with a deliberate roll of his eyes. "Jillian has you wrapped around her finger, and you've become a besotted fool."

Dean didn't even deny it, but also couldn't pass up the opportunity to get in a dig of his own. "At least I'm getting it on a regular basis, with a wife who has become game for just about anything. It's a great place to be."

"Don't worry about me," Mac drawled. "I get it as often as I want it, with women who

ERIKA WILDE

are just as accommodating as I need them to be."

Mac sounded convincing, but Dean new better. Ever since Mac's divorce, he'd kept all women at an emotional distance and indulged in short-lived affairs with females who enjoyed the level of kink that he did. But knowing Mac as well as he did, Dean suspected that those meaningless encounters were starting to lose their appeal.

Knowing it was a realization his friend had to figure out for himself, Dean changed the subject. "I want to let you know that I'll be out of town next weekend, from Friday through Monday. I made sure there's nothing conflicting on the schedule, so if you'll be on call until I return, I'd appreciate it."

"Sure thing," Mac replied then raised a curious brow. "I take it you have something planned with Jillian?"

"I do. She just doesn't know it yet." Dean grinned. "I'm going to surprise her."

Mac tipped his head. "I can't imagine that anything could top the surprise of you taking her to The Players Club for your twentieth anniversary."

THE CAPTURE

That evening at the exclusive sex club with Jillian brought back very fond and erotic memories for Dean. "Honestly, I didn't either, until I was in New York last month having dinner with Gabe Dare," he said of one of their high profile clients on the East coast that they did occasional security work for. "He'd just gotten back from a place called Eden, a private island and resort located off of Florida in the Bermuda Triangle region."

"The Bermuda Triangle?" Mac frowned, his gaze glimmering with concern. "That sounds . . . ominous."

Dean laughed. "Gabe and Isabelle, his fiancée, returned to the states just fine," he assured his friend. "From what Gabe told me, and the information I received, Eden is like a fantasy island, where anything goes and guests are transported to whatever kind of adventure they request. I thought it would be a fun get-away for Jillian and me."

Mac smirked. "Upon arrival, will you be greeted by Mr. Roarke and his side-kick, Tattoo?" he said, referencing the old, iconic television series *Fantasy Island*.

Dean pitched a paperclip at his friend,

5

which bounced right off Mac's chest. "I'll let you know, *smart-ass*."

"*If* you find your way back *out* of the Bermuda Triangle," Mac said, humor lacing his voice. "So, what kind of adventure do you have in mind for yourself and Jillian?"

"That's between me and my wife." Dean wasn't about to share the details of Jillian's intimate fantasy, mainly because he *knew* that Mac would give him shit about what he had planned, and just how far he intended to go to fulfill one of her secret desires. He'd never live it down if Mac knew all the elaborate details.

"Must be something *really* good," Mac said as he stood up to leave. "If you're not back by that Tuesday, do you want me to send the Special Forces into the Bermuda Triangle to find and extract you and Jillian?"

"You're such a comedian," Dean said drolly, so *not* amused by Mac's attempt at humor. "Now get the fuck out of my office."

Mac headed out the door, his unoffended laughter following him into his own office across the hall.

# CHAPTER 2

"Hey, Jillian, a courier just dropped off an envelope for you."

Jillian glanced up from the swatches of fabric spread out on the work table in the design studio for Fantasy Bedrooms as the owner, Stephanie, approached with a flat parcel in hand. Stephanie was also her boss, as well as a good friend, and there wasn't a day that went by that Jillian wasn't grateful that the other woman had offered her a job as an assistant designer. Not because Jillian needed the money, but because she was at a point in her life, with both of her sons grown

ERIKA WILDE

and gone, that she'd desperately needed a creative outlet of her own.

Broaching the subject of working with Dean had shaken the foundation of their marriage, but she'd stood her ground despite her husband's stubborn ultimatum, and their relationship was stronger and more balanced as a result of her determination and fortitude.

Since she hadn't been expecting any kind of delivery, Jillian asked, "Who is it from?"

"I have no idea," Stephanie said as she handed over the flat, thin envelope. "There isn't a return name or address."

"Well, that makes me a little nervous," she murmured, even as she ripped open the tab securing the flap and withdrew the contents —a folded piece of stationary and another sealed envelope. As soon as she unfolded the cream colored sheet of paper, she recognized the logo for Noble and Associates embossed at the top, as well as her husband's handwriting as she began reading his note.

Jillian,

You're mine for the weekend.

Enclosed you will find an envelope with a

THE CAPTURE

plane ticket to Florida inside, along with brief instructions on what to do once you get there. Outside, a Town Car is waiting to take you to the airport. There is nothing you need to bring with you. I will make sure you have everything you need when you get to your destination, where I will meet up with you when it's time.

Enjoy your fantasy.

Love,
Dean

Excitement jump started the wild beat of her heart, but the initial thrill of Dean's spontaneous letter, and the ensuing adventure he'd planned, warred with other responsibilities and obligations. It was Friday morning, she'd just gotten to the office, and she couldn't just up and leave work on a whim. She thought he'd come to understand how important her job was to her, and she wasn't happy that he'd put her in such an awkward situation.

"Everything okay?" Stephanie asked.

Jillian exhaled a frustrated stream of

breath and glanced at her boss. "Dean wants to go away for the weekend. Starting right this minute. I can't believe he set all this up without talking to me first. I can't just walk out-"

"Yes, you can," her friend interrupted with a grin. "Dean called me about a week ago to ask if you could have this weekend off because he had a surprise get-away in mind. He wanted to make sure there wasn't any work related conflicts, or anything important you needed to be here for, and there *isn't*, so I wasn't about to say no to something so romantic."

Jillian raised a brow. "So, you knew all about this?"

Stephanie shrugged. "I knew he had something planned for the weekend, but I don't know details."

"Neither do I," she said wryly as she skimmed the letter from Dean again. "It's all very mysterious. I've got a plane ticket to Florida, and a note stating not to pack anything because he'll have everything taken care of when I get to wherever I'm going."

"Maybe he's taking you to one of those

THE CAPTURE

clothing optional resorts," Stephanie suggested.

Jillian cringed at the thought. "Umm, no. Just . . . *no*." She laughed out loud and shook her head. "Walking around completely naked in front of other people is way beyond my comfort zone." And since Dean had signed the letter with *enjoy your fantasy*, she was inclined to believe that whatever lay ahead had been planned with deliberate care, attention to detail, and her own personal fantasies in mind, which he knew intimately.

"Whatever is awaiting you, I'm sure it's going to be sexy and fun, so go and enjoy yourself," Stephanie said.

"Are you absolutely sure?" Jillian asked, wanting to be certain that she wasn't leaving her boss short-handed.

"Of course I am," her friend said as she retrieved Jillian's purse from the cubby next to the drafting table. "Anything that needs to be done in regards to the Miller's playroom you're designing can wait until next week, or I can take care of myself." She pushed the leather bag into Jillian's hands. "Now get out of here and that's an order. Your car is

ERIKA WILDE

waiting out front to whisk you away for a weekend with your gorgeous husband, you lucky girl."

"I won't argue with that. I'm a *very* lucky girl." Tucking her husband's letter and her plane ticket to Florida into her purse, she slung it over her shoulder and headed toward the front door of the office.

Knowing she had her boss's blessing allowed Jillian to enjoy the sense of anticipation rushing through her as she made her way outside and was greeted by the suit clad driver, who stood by the open back door of a shiny black Town Car. With a wave to Stephanie, she slid inside the vehicle and let the gentleman close the door after her.

As they drove toward the San Diego International airport, Jillian stared out the window at the passing scenery, thinking about how far she and Dean had come in their marriage and relationship in the past year. Seducing him in his office that day, and voicing her more forbidden desires to her husband, had changed their routine sex life into hot, erotic encounters that just kept on getting better and better.

THE CAPTURE

But, admittedly, it had taken a lot of communication and compromise to get to this great point in their marriage, and it wasn't very long ago that she'd rocked the boat, so to speak, by announcing her intention of going to work after being a wife and stay-at-home mom for twenty years. Her need to do something for herself had gone against Dean's deep-seated duty to provide completely for his wife and family, which all stemmed from his own childhood and growing up with a drunken father who hadn't given a damn about his wife or son.

They'd managed to work through that stumbling block in their relationship, and even though Dean would always prefer that she didn't work so he could take care of her the way a husband should, he now understood her reasons for wanting a career of her own and supported her decision.

While she loved being a decorator for Fantasy Bedrooms and would never give up her job, over the past few months she'd discovered just how difficult it was to balance work and more intimate time with Dean—especially considering his erratic

13

schedule and frequent business trips as a security consultant for his own firm—and just how hard it was to keep things fresh and exciting in the bedroom. Lately, they'd both been working long hours and were too tired in the evenings to indulge in some of their favorite past-times in their personal play-room, and she missed those more erotic, kinky encounters with her husband.

Apparently, Dean was feeling the same way, and she was dying to know what kind of hot and dirty fantasy he'd arranged for the two of them to enjoy.

The Town Car pulled up to the curb at the airport, and the journey began. She checked in with the airlines, delighted to discover that Dean had purchased a seat for her in first class. She had just enough time to get through security and purchase a book to read on the flight before boarding the plane.

The day consisted of eight hours of travel with a short lay-over in Houston where she grabbed a quick sandwich to take with her on the next leg of her flight, and finally arrived in Miami, Florida, at five in the afternoon. As she followed the rest of the travelers down to

THE CAPTURE

the transportation area of the airport, she saw a pretty young woman in her mid-twenties holding up a sign with her name, JILLIAN NOBLE, in bold text – just as Dean's brief instructions told her she would.

Jillian approached the woman with a smile. "Hi. I'm Jillian. You must be Joely. My husband, Dean, said you'd be taking me to wherever my final destination will be."

The younger woman's green eyes lit up. "Yes, I'm Joely," she confirmed. "It's so nice to meet you. I'll be providing your transportation to Eden."

Eden—Jillian's first clue as to where she was going. She'd never heard of such a place before, though the name alone made it sound very appealing. She fell into step beside her escort and slipped into a waiting vehicle. She expected a short drive to this place called Eden, but instead they arrived at a marina with a seaplane docked at the end of a pier.

"Is that plane for us?" Jillian asked hesitantly as she and Joely got out of the car and headed toward the small aircraft.

"Yes. It's the quickest way to get to Eden." Joely must have seen the nervous look on

15

Jillian's face because she rushed to reassure her. "Don't worry. You're in safe hands. I'm a former bush pilot and I've been chartering guests to the island of Eden for years."

Jillian had no choice but to trust the other woman, as well as Dean since he undoubtedly knew she'd have to fly in this tiny plane. "What is Eden, other than an island?" she asked curiously as she climbed into the back and settled into a small seat next to the window, hoping to get a better idea of where she was headed.

"It's a very magical place, located in the Bermuda Triangle," her pilot said as she took her own seat in the cockpit, then glanced back at Jillian with a grin. "Eden is anything you want it to be."

The last part of her comment sounded enticing, but Jillian could only wrap her mind around one thing. "The Bermuda Triangle?" she repeated, unable to keep the trepidation from her voice.

Joely just laughed, as if Jillian's reaction was a common one. "Don't panic. We haven't lost a guest yet." She powered up the plane and flipped some switches on the panel in

THE CAPTURE

front of her. "Put your headset on, relax, and enjoy the ride and view."

Between the small plane and them heading toward the Bermuda Triangle, Jillian didn't think she *could* fully relax, but Joely proved to be an exceptional pilot and the ride was smooth and uneventful.

"We're nearly there," Joely said almost two hours later, the microphone on her headset linked to Jillian's. "Look out your window. The view of Eden from up here is breath-taking and you don't want to miss it."

For the first time since taking off, Jillian glanced down, catching a glimpse of a stunningly lush and gorgeous island out in the middle of the Atlantic Ocean as Joely landed the plane on the water and taxied toward a small pier. Dominating the piece of land was an enormous, majestic-looking Irish castle made of gray stone that looked to be centuries old. With the sun setting behind the massive palace, the entire structure seemed to shimmer with a life of its own.

It certainly wasn't your normal island resort, and Jillian was both intrigued and

17

ERIKA WILDE

enchanted by the castle, and what might lie ahead.

She and Joely stepped out of the plane, and Jillian frowned when she saw a man at the end of the dock, wearing all black, with a cloak and a hood obscuring his face. He stood with his hands behind his back, legs slightly apart, his entire presence commanding and compelling.

"Who is that?" she whispered to the younger woman as they walked toward him.

"He is the Master of the island," Joely replied simply. "He likes to greet his guests as they arrive, when he's able to."

They reached the man, and he extended a hand toward Jillian, and she slipped her palm into his larger, stronger one. "You must be Jillian," he said, his deep voice just as mysterious as his persona. "Welcome to Eden, where reality is whatever you wish it to be."

She smiled, remembering that Joely had said the same thing about this island. "That's quite a promise."

He tipped his hooded head in amusement. "I guess you'll just have to see and experience it for yourself." He turned and signaled for a

THE CAPTURE

young blonde-haired woman standing a few feet away from him, dressed in simple silk khaki drawstring pants and a white sleeveless top that appeared to be the island's uniform. "Leila will show you your accommodations and take care of anything you should want or need."

"Thank you." Jillian followed the other woman along the pathway leading to the castle, then up a series of stone steps. Once inside, her decorator's eye took in the fixtures and furnishings, from the rich marble flooring to the overhead chandeliers dripping with cut crystals. The interior had been restored to reflect the age and beauty of the castle, along with a few modern upgrades, but there was no mistaking the mystical, magical feel of the place.

"Right this way," Leila said, and led her down a corridor until they arrived at a door, which she opened and Jillian followed her into a spacious, luxurious bedroom decorated in soothing colors of white and gray, and accented with deep purple—again, much more contemporary and stylish than she'd expected.

ERIKA WILDE

"This is where you'll be staying the night," the younger woman told her. "There are toiletries in the adjoining bathroom, and a brand new silk chemise and robe on the bed for you to sleep in. If you need anything at all, just pick up the telephone and make your request. Your dinner should arrive within the hour."

Jillian turned to Leila with a smile. "It's all very lovely. Thank you."

"You're very welcome," she replied, a delighted sparkle in her eyes. "Your fantasy will begin in the morning at ten am, after you've had breakfast." She headed back toward the door, then stopped and glanced back. "Oh, and those flowers on the dresser were delivered specifically for you."

Once Leila was gone, Jillian strolled over to the vibrant bouquet of exotic flowers arranged in a cut crystal vase and removed the attached card. She opened the envelope and read the message from Dean.

*I hope you enjoy your accommodations tonight. Sleep well and I'll see you tomorrow.*

Jillian felt a pang of disappointment that she wasn't going to be sharing this first night

THE CAPTURE

in Eden with her husband. And there was absolutely no hint of what he had planned for her in the brief note. The anticipation was killing her, but she was certain that was exactly what her husband had intended.

# CHAPTER 3

*J*illian woke up the following morning feeling more rested and refreshed than she had in a very long time—despite the long, exhausting day of travel the previous day. She was also excited to see Dean and finally find out what fantasy awaited her.

She was sitting out on the balcony overlooking what she could see of the beautiful, lush island and deep blue ocean, and had just finished eating a continental breakfast with the most delicious fruit and pastries, when a knock sounded on the door—precisely at 10 am, as Leila had stated.

Still wearing the chemise she'd slept in—

THE CAPTURE

because she had nothing else to wear except yesterday's outfit—she covered up with the matching robe and went to the door. A sweet, elderly woman stood on the other side, her brown eyes bright and cheerful.

"Good morning, Mistress," she said with a polite nod of her head. "I'll be taking you to the spa to ready you for your new Master."

*New Master?* A flutter of excitement stirred inside of her. Knowing this was all part of Dean's arrangement, she followed the woman to another part of the castle and into a private spa where three other young girls were waiting to proceed with an abundance of beauty treatments.

Over the next three hours, Jillian was pampered from head-to-toe. She was waxed and plucked, *everywhere*, then moved on to a facial while two of the girls gave her a manicure and pedicure. Her skin was exfoliated with a sea salt scrub until it was baby soft, then she was massaged and rubbed down with soothing, fragrant oils. Her hair was washed, dried, and curled into loose waves, and a light dusting of make-up enhanced her now glowing complexion.

ERIKA WILDE

"All that's left is to get you dressed," one of the girls, Claire, said as she ushered Jillian into a smaller, adjoining room with a full length mirror, and pieces of clothing hanging from a few pegs on the wall that had a costume feel to them.

Claire stood there, waiting for Jillian to take off the silk robe, and she smiled at the younger woman. "I think I can manage to get dressed on my own."

"My job is to help, and you might have some trouble with the ties."

Jillian didn't know what "ties" the girl was referring to, but considering Claire had already seen Jillian naked in the spa, she stripped off the robe and let the girl do her job. Turning Jillian away from the mirror, Claire removed a white cotton blouse from a hanger and pulled it over her head, followed by helping her step into a flowing black skirt that fell to her calves but had a side slit on the left side that reached all the way up to her upper thigh and exposed the length of her leg.

Jillian was all too aware of the fact that she didn't have any underwear on beneath

THE CAPTURE

the blouse and skirt—especially the blouse, since it was pulled tight across her breasts and she could see her own nipples through the thin, white fabric. "Umm, I think you forgot my bra and panties."

"No, Mistress," Claire said, amusement in her voice as she reached for what looked like a very wide belt and wrapped it around Jillian's waist with the two ends meeting in the front. "I was instructed to make sure you didn't wear any."

"Oh." *Dean's* instructions, no doubt, she thought, her cheeks warming in realization.

Claire ducked her head, hiding her smile as she started lacing up the front of what appeared to be an under-the-bust corset in a gorgeous red brocade. The other woman pulled the silk ribbons tight, cinching in Jillian's waist with the steel boning and plumping up her breasts over the top edge. When she was done with the bindings, she adjusted the sleeves of Jillian's blouse off her arms, then helped her into a pair of shiny, black, knee-length, patent leather boots with a three inch heel.

Finished dressing Jillian, Claire turned

her back around so she could see her reflection in the mirror.

Jillian inhaled a startled breath, barely recognizing the wanton woman staring back at her. Her lustrous hair fell around her bare shoulders, framing the ample cleavage spilling indecently from the low, tight bodice of her blouse. The corset gave her curves a voluptuous, hour-glass shape, and if she wasn't careful with the way she walked, the high slit in her skirt had the potential of flashing her girly-bits to anyone looking her way. The sexy, *fuck-me* boots laced up the sides and completed the seductive ensemble.

"I think you're going to cause quite the commotion with all those randy sailors at the auction today."

Claire's comment pulled Jillian's attention back to the other woman. "Auction?"

"Yes, Mistress," she said with a nod of her head. "Samson sells all the wenches he kidnaps to the highest bidder. It's rumored that the notorious Black Heart will be there. Men fear him, and women revere him because he's known for his insatiable sexual appetite."

*Oh, my.* Jillian's mind raced as she realized which fantasy of hers Dean was creating —being taken by a dominant, rogue of a pirate. While she was certainly dressed the part of a *wench*, she had no idea what was about to transpire, but the thought of being ravished and plundered by a swashbuckling outlaw sent a secret, illicit thrill arcing through her, especially if *Dean* was Black Heart.

A door behind her opened and an older man with a weathered face and gray grizzly beard strode in, dressed in tattered pirate garb. He held a coiled length of rope in one hand, and an old pistol was tucked into the belt wrapped around his waist.

"I've come to fetch the dame," he said, his voice gruff and slightly accented. "Is she ready?"

"Yes, sir," Claire responded, and stepped aside so the older man could approach Jillian.

He stopped a few feet away, his narrowed eyes assessing all of her, seemingly pleased with what he saw. "What a bonny wench you are. You should bring in a tidy sum at the auction. These sailors have been at sea for months and are hungry for a taste of something sweet like you."

He walked behind her and gathered both of Jillian's hands at the base of her spine. As soon as she felt him wrap the soft hewn rope around her wrists, she had a moment of uncertainty as fantasy blurred with reality, and her gaze sought Claire's.

The other woman must have sensed her panic, because Claire was quick to offer a reassurance. "Your safe word applies at all times."

Claire's statement automatically calmed her, and let her know that Dean was truly orchestrating this entire scenario, even if he wasn't present at the moment. Knowing she had that safeguard in place allowed her to slip into character and enjoy the fantasy.

Once Samson had her hands secured, he grabbed her arm and led her through the door he'd just entered. As soon as they stepped through, Jillian noticed an immediate change . . . the corridor, made up of faded red brick, was cool and damp, with sconces lighting the way. As they neared the end of the tunnel, the sound of lyrical music,

THE CAPTURE

as well as loud, raucous laughter and general merriment grew louder, until the passageway opened into what appeared to be an old-time alehouse. The pub was filled with sailors and pirates who were drinking ale and rum, and chasing the tavern maids who didn't seem to mind being man-handled, if their bawdy laughter was anything to go by.

It all looked and felt so real, as if she'd been transported back to Tortuga in the 1700's. Samson led her up three steps to a wooden platform, *clearly an auction block*, that overlooked the entire establishment and put her on display. The place immediately quieted down, and the men in the pub shifted their attention to her. With her hands still tied behind her back, and Samson holding the end of the rope, Jillian had no choice but to stand in front of the entire tavern and endure all the lewd and lascivious stares.

She searched the place for Dean, but couldn't find him anywhere.

A male voice from the crowd yelled out, "What do you have for us there, Samson?"

"The finest wench gold can buy, to do with as you please," he replied in that gruff

29

ERIKA WILDE

voice of his. "Her hair's like silk and her skin is soft and supple. Just look at that lush mouth and those firm tits, so don't be stingy with your coins. Who'll put up the first bid for this fine piece of female flesh?"

Samson's prompting was all it took for the sailors and pirates to start yelling out different sums of gold and silver, each one topping the previous amount. The men turned aggressive and contentious as they battled it out for supremacy, and as the bids climbed higher and higher, so did the anxious sensation swirling in the pit of Jillian's stomach because she suddenly felt very vulnerable. Here she was, shackled and in a strange place, and the rabid men in the tavern were eyeing her hungrily as they vied to purchase her—what if one them actually *won* her?

She swallowed hard at the thought, feeling a bit dizzy by the crazy bidding war going on in front of her.

"Going once to Captain Howell," Sampson called out once the bidding reach a staggering amount that no one else could afford to top.

Captain Howell, confident in his win, stepped forward to claim her. He looked reminiscent of Johnny Depp's character as Jack Sparrow in The Pirates of the Caribbean —complete with his hair in dreadlocks with beads and feathers, a braided goatee, and well-worn pirate garb. A small knife was sheathed to his belt, and when he smiled wolfishly, his gold front tooth glimmered. He appeared *very* adept at pillaging and plundering.

"Going twice to Captain Howell . . ."

Jillian's heart pounded frantically in her chest as Sampson opened his mouth to award the man his prize . . . *her.*

"I will *double* the amount of anyone's bid," came a familiar male voice before the auctioneer spoke those final words. "The wench is my slave and will belong to me."

A tavern maid standing near the stage gasped in awe. "Oh, my God, it's *Black Heart.*"

From a shadowed corner of the pub, Dean —or rather, Black Heart—stepped out and strolled confidently toward the platform, and Jillian's knees nearly buckled in relief. The other men backed away, except for the Jack

Sparrow look-alike who held his position, while the women in the room stared at the approaching rogue with envy and pure, unadulterated lust.

His presence was undeniably commanding. While the rest of the pirates in the tavern looked weathered by months at sea, Black Heart looked stunningly gorgeous and noble in a loose, white, long-sleeved shirt, a black embroidered waistcoat, and tight black breeches that hugged his lean hips and strong thighs and tucked into a pair of shiny black leather boots.

Howell puffed out his chest and glared belligerently at Black Heart. "Back down," he said sternly. "Samson was just about to award her to me."

Black Heart gave the other man a calloused look. "He did not finalize the bid, therefore I believe I topped your price, as well as everyone else's in this tavern."

The other man put his hand on the small knife at his waist. "Are you challenging me?"

"I will challenge *anyone* in order to claim her," Black Heart said, and wrapped his fingers around the jeweled handle of the

THE CAPTURE

much larger and more lethal sword sheathed at his side.

The whole exchange was so sexy and barbaric, Jillian had to suppress the urge to swoon—and quickly reminded herself that in this fantasy, this dark and dangerous pirate who wanted her as a *slave* was the enemy, not her savior.

"Don't be stupid, Howell," Samson barked out. "This man's ruthless reputation precedes him. Do you wish to die tonight?"

Howell stood his ground for a few more seconds then begrudgingly walked away, conceding defeat. Once he was gone, Black Heart casually made his way up to the small dais, looming large as he stopped in front of Jillian, making her very aware of the fact that they still had an audience below. Refusing to fall to his feet in servitude, she pushed back her shoulders and lifted her chin in a show of defiance.

His heated gaze dropped to the full, generous breasts nearly overflowing her blouse from the stays in her corset, then traveled up to her lips. Threading his fingers tight into her hair until it was wrapped

ERIKA WILDE

around his wrist, he pulled her head back so that she was forced to look up at him. His eyes burned with desire, and without warning he crushed his mouth to hers in a kiss that was hot, hard, and unapologetically dominating—claiming her for all to witness, in the most basic, primal way possible.

His wide shoulders blocked her view of everyone else, but she could hear the women cheering and the male patrons tossing out cat-calls and bawdy comments to egg him on. Despite being on display, a thrill shot through her, pooling into liquid heat between her legs—and still he wasn't done marking her, branding her as his. His hand boldly slid into the high opening in her skirt and skimmed up her thigh, his tongue delving deeper into her mouth just as he touched her bare, freshly waxed pussy and slid two fingers between the lips of her sex.

Her body jolted at his indecent caress, and a possessive growl erupted from his throat as he wedged a booted foot between hers and forced her to widen her stance, giving him complete access to her. He pushed one finger,

THE CAPTURE

then two, deep into her slick channel and brushed his thumb across her clit.

She hated herself for groaning, for shuddering, for nearly melting at the skillful way he fucked her with his fingers and rubbed against that sensitive spot inside of her that threatened to tip her over into a screaming orgasm. With her hands bound behind her back, and his fingers gripping her hair, she was at his sweet, decadent mercy, and he had no qualms about taking advantage of that fact.

With concentrated effort, she once again lectured herself that she was supposed to resist this man who'd just bought her, this rake of a pirate who intended to use her as his slave to slake his physical needs and lust. Tugging her head back from his tight hold on her hair, she put up a decent struggle to pull her mouth away, and he ended the kiss, though she knew it was only because *he'd* wanted the kiss to end. There was no doubt in her mind that he could easily overpower her if he wanted to.

He withdrew his fingers slowly from her body. His eyes were dark and so hot as they

ERIKA WILDE

stared into hers that she felt singed, every-where. "I'm not sure what I'll enjoy fucking first," he mused, a wicked smile curving his full, sensual lips. "Your mouth, your tits, or your soft, warm cunt."

He'd loosened his hold on her hair to allow just enough slack that she was able to unexpectedly nip at his lower lip with her teeth—not hard enough to break the skin, but definitely firm enough to illicit a sting of pain and show him she wasn't docile or submissive.

He instinctively jerked back and rubbed his thumb across his bottom lip where she'd assaulted him, clearly shocked by her audacity—and more than a little turned on by the challenge she presented, if the amuse-ment filling his gaze was anything to go by.

"This one is full of fire," Samson said around a bellowing laugh. "You'll get your money's worth with her, and more."

"Aye," Black Heart agreed, the pirate slang sounding so incredibly sexy coming from his lips. "I'm counting on it. I like my women spirited. Makes the surrender all the more satisfying."

THE CAPTURE

She jutted her chin out rebelliously. "I will never surrender to the likes of you!"

"Mark my words, slave. You *will* yield and submit, and enjoy doing so." He took the ropes securing her wrists from Samson and wrapped the ends around his strong hand. "I've been at sea for months, and it's been too long since my cock has been buried in a woman's soft heat, and yours is ripe for plundering."

The bawdy sailors cheered him on with lewd comments and encouragements and Jillian's cheeks flushed pink at all the obscenely sexual suggestions being shouted their way.

Through it all, she managed to maintain a bit of sass. "You're much too sure of yourself and your charms," she said brazenly.

"Aye, I am." He flashed her a cocky, confident grin as he grabbed her arm and guided her down the wooden steps. "Let's go, wench. I have plans for you that don't include exhibitionism. At least not yet," he added shamelessly.

37

# CHAPTER 4

*H*er dashing, scoundrel of a pirate led her through a part of Eden that was lush and beautiful, and seemingly deserted, until they reached a cottage built out of large, smooth stones, with moss on the roof and vines climbing along the sides. He opened the door and gently pushed her inside, then followed behind her. As he untied the rope from the hands still secured behind her back, she glanced around the small but spacious place, which was decorated in rich shades of burgundy and gold.

A huge four-poster bed dominated the main room, and off to the side was a rustic,

THE CAPTURE

hand-carved table with two chairs and a wood burning stove to give off heat, if needed. An open door led to a more modern looking bathroom, and there was another door, painted bright red, that remained closed.

As soon as her hands were freed, she rubbed at her wrists, while Black Heart moved toward the massive bed and removed his belt and sword, then started unbuttoning his waistcoat.

"Get undressed and get on the bed, slave," he demanded, his tone brusque.

Clearly, he was anxious to get down to business and expected her to obey his command, but she wasn't about to make any of this easy on him. He tossed the embroidered vest onto a chair next to the bed, and when he turned away to pull the loose white shirt over his head, it gave her a few precious moments to execute her very spontaneous plan to escape.

Whirling around, she flung the door open and ran, following a dirt path that led her further and deeper into the forest, her long hair flying out behind her. She heard him

ERIKA WILDE

swear, heard his booted footsteps on the wooden floor of the cottage, then the sound of him running after her.

Her pulse leapt in her throat, the thrill of the chase mingling with the trepidation of what he'd do to her once he caught her . . . which she knew he would. He was bigger, stronger, and faster, and Black Heart didn't seem like a man who tolerated disobedience without due punishment.

The heavy weight of her skirt tangling around her legs and the high heels on her boots hindered her speed and agility. Her heart raced wildly in her chest as the sound of his approach grew louder, and she let out a yelp of pain as his hand closed around her loose hair, jerking her backward and throwing her off balance.

She stumbled and started to fall, and he wrapped a strong arm around her waist as he tackled her to a patch of soft moss. He took the brunt of the fall so that she fell on top of him, but he quickly reversed their positions, rolling them both so that she was sprawled beneath him.

In a quick, lithe move, he straddled her

THE CAPTURE

hips with his powerful thighs, but her arms were free and she used them to try and shove at his chest while bucking her hips in hopes of dismounting him.

*Yeah, right*, as if that was even possible. The man was solid muscle, and his thighs were like vice clamps, pinning her in place despite her struggles.

His gray eyes caught fire, their tussle clearly arousing him. Much too effortlessly he caught her wrists and held them bound in his hands. Sitting atop her, he looked formidable and intimidating, and devastatingly gorgeous. His dark hair was disheveled, the soft sable strands falling rakishly across his forehead. His broad chest was bare, his skin tan and taut. The muscles in his arms and across his abdomen flexed with the barest movement. Those tight black breeches encased his toned, sinewy thighs, and outlined the hard, impressive length of his cock.

She was breathing hard, and his gaze settled on her heaving chest and the unbound breasts rising and falling beneath her white blouse before lifting to meet her eyes. He

41

ERIKA WILDE

arched a dark brow, his expression arrogant and mocking. "Did you really think you could escape me?"

"Did you think I would submit to you so easily?" she retorted impudently. "I am no man's slave!"

He laughed, the low, rumbling sound vibrating from his body, to hers, making her nipples peak tight and hard. "You're bought and paid for, wench. You belong to me."

She thrashed beneath him and tried to yank her hands from his unrelenting grasp, all to no avail. "I belong to no man!"

He smirked, so confident in his superior position as he pinned her arms above her head and leaned over her, causing his stiff erection to rub oh-so-deliciously against her mound. Even through their clothing she could feel him, so thick and long and hard, and her traitorous body responded with a rush of wet heat between her legs.

As if he could scent her arousal, his nostrils flared and his eyes darkened to slate. "I guess I'll just have to prove to you that I *am* your Master."

She knew his words weren't a mere threat

THE CAPTURE

to make her obey, they were a promise, and she couldn't suppress the secret thrill that coursed through her, even as she dared to defy him with a willful toss of her head. "Do you intend to claim me, right here and now?"

"Oh, no," he murmured, his silky smooth voice like a caress to her senses. "I'm definitely tempted, but tonight you're going to learn a very important lesson. That you are *mine*. You will be whatever I want you to be. You will do whatever I ask you to, or suffer the consequences. And starting right now, I'm going to show you exactly how I deal with a slave's insubordination."

With a stunning grace and agility, he quickly rose to his booted feet, tugging on her wrists as he stood so that she was pulled up, too. Before she could gain her bearings, he hefted her over his shoulder like a sack of potatoes and locked his arm around the back of her legs, while her upper body hung down his back, her loose hair nearly reaching the mossy ground.

"You're a barbarian!" she said, trying to kick her feet, which merely bounced off his taut stomach.

43

"Aye, you have no idea how barbaric I'm about to get, wench." He slid a hand up her skirt, his hot palm traveling all the way up to her bare ass. He pinched her cheek and she yelped in surprise, and his satisfied chuckle reached her ears.

She wasn't even close to being small and petite, but he carried her without effort or strain, the muscles across his shoulders and down his bare back flexing with each step he took. She was dizzy from dangling upside down, but at least she had a view of his gorgeous, tight ass encased in his breeches, and damned if her hands didn't itch to smack his firm, sinewy buttocks, but resisted the impulse since she knew his own retribution would be swift and painful since he had the upper hand.

He finally reached the cottage and once they were inside he locked the door this time. He didn't put her down, but instead walked to that mysterious red door, opened it, and strode into the quarters.

The interior was cool and dim, and considering her upside-down position, it was difficult to really see what was in the room.

THE CAPTURE

He finally set her on her feet, and since her head was spinning and her equilibrium was momentarily skewed, he definitely had the advantage and didn't hesitate to take advantage of that fact. He secured a soft leather cuff around each of her wrists, then pulled on a nearby chain that stretched her arms straight above her head, leaving her defenseless and completely vulnerable to whatever he decided to do to her.

She blinked, and her eyes finally adjusted to the low lighting, revealing her surroundings, which looked like a BDSM dungeon. There were no windows, just sconces on the walls to provide the only illumination in the chamber, glinting off the long chains and restraints hanging from the walls and ceiling. There were padded benches, tables with straps, and a wooden St. Andrew's cross positioned in the far corner—furniture designed for pleasure, or pain, depending on the user's intent.

Her wicked pirate turned around and opened a nearby cabinet displaying a wide range of crops, whips, canes, and other disciplinary devices. After a long moment of

ERIKA WILDE

contemplation that heightened the anticipation swirling inside of her, he made his selection and returned to her suspended form. He stood in front of her, booted feet braced apart and a hedonistic smile on his lips as he threaded the long, individual tassels of a flogger through his fingers, caressing the strands like a lover.

She'd swallowed hard and met his searing gaze. "What are you going to do to me?"

"I'm going to teach you a lesson," he drawled, and set the whip on a table close to him, along with two small items that gleamed silver and red. "I believe you called me barbaric, and I certainly don't want to disappoint you."

He reached down and retrieved a small jewel-handled knife from his boot, then positioned the sharp blade against the ties securing the front of her corset and expertly cut them away. She sucked in a startled breath as the bustier fell to the floor, and gasped again when he made a slice in her shirt, then savagely ripped it apart with his bare hands so that it hung from both of her shoulders and left her entire upper body

46

THE CAPTURE

naked to his gaze. He stripped her skirt down her legs and tossed it aside, baring the rest of her, but left her boots intact.

He straightened once again, slowly sliding the dull edge of the knife up her inner thigh, along her belly, around the curve of one breast, and scraped it over a rigid nipple. Her entire body jolted at the twinge of pain that shot through her, and a low moan escaped her throat.

"*No,*" she said, and thrashed for freedom, which did no good.

"Oh, *Yes,*" he murmured insolently, his expression filled with depraved lust. "You were bought for my pleasure, and I'm going to show you that I can fuck you any way I want, and any time I desire. And maybe, if you're a good slave and do as you're told, there might be pleasure in it for you, too. Eventually, once you learn to submit to me."

She lifted her chin, displaying her pride, which was all she had left at the moment. "It will *never* happen."

"Oh, mark my words, it most definitely *will* happen, and I'll enjoy making you scream, and beg. Repeatedly."

ERIKA WILDE

She pursed her lips at his vanity. "You're an arrogant libertine!"

He chuckled at her insult. "Aye, I suppose I am."

Setting the knife aside, he filled his palms with her breasts, squeezing them together and flicking a finger over her taut nipples. "Such gorgeous, lush tits," he murmured, and bent his head, pulling one breast into his mouth, sucking hard and deep. His tongue swirled around the areola, and his teeth tugged relentlessly on the aching peak.

Her sex clenched in response, and that fast, she was close to screaming and begging. Instead, she bit her bottom lip and swallowed a moan, determined not to give him the satisfaction of hearing her cries of pleasure.

He performed the same treatment on her other breast—licking, sucking, and biting— while his hands fondled and his fingers twisted her nipples until they were so hard and sensitive they hurt-so-good. Her breathing was harsh, her lips parted, the word *please* desperate to escape, yet somehow she managed to remain quiet.

"Aye, you *are* a stubborn one," he said,

THE CAPTURE

amusement softening his tone as he *finally* released her breasts and lifted his head to look at her. He reached for those red and silver things he'd put on the table. "Let's see if I can get a reaction out of you with these."

*These* were nipple clamps with a large, teardrop ruby for added pull once they were secured. He clipped the silver vices on each of her stiff nipples, the weight of the gemstone escalating the sensitivity in her nipples and creating an intensifying sensation she felt all the way down to her pussy. The slightest movement caused the rubies to sway, and the pressure blossomed into a titillating ache she could barely keep contained.

"So fucking beautiful," he said, stepping back so he could rake his gaze down the length of her—from the arms stretched above her head, the hair spilling over her shoulders, to her bejeweled breasts, all the way down to her throbbing sex.

He picked up the flogger once again, stroking the strips of suede. "Are you ready for your punishment, for ignoring my order to strip and get on the bed, and running

ERIKA WILDE

instead? Or would you rather beg for mercy?"

The word *mercy* caught her attention, a safe word that had been established months ago that her pirate was giving her the option to use now. "I will not beg," she told him, and watched his dark eyes flash with male gratification.

"Very well." He moved to stand behind her, lightly stroking his fingers down the slope of her spine and over her buttocks, creating goose bumps all over her skin. "You will receive twenty lashes for your disobedience. I am your Master, and you *will* learn to obey me."

His touch fell away and was replaced by the first snap of thin suede strips connecting against her exposed flesh. She gasped and arched at the bite of pain, and with each lash on her backside, her ass, her thighs, the sting became a stroke, and every affliction became a yearning for more.

It was pure, sweet agony.

The moans she tried so hard to keep in check finally broke free, the sensual sound

THE CAPTURE

shocking her with the depth of desire and need he evoked with every crack of his multi-strand whip. Her head fell forward, and she shuddered as he landed another blow that caused the suede strips to wrap around her upper thigh, and the tips of the flogger to tap across her mound in a way that made her knees go weak.

He strolled around to stand in front of her again, continuing the delicious torment on her front-side—lashing the upper swells of her tender breasts, her belly, her legs— wielding the flogger in such a skillful way that created a delicious burning warmth to spread across her skin, and dissolve into something perfectly, breath-takingly exquisite.

The scene was kinky, undignified, and Lord help her, *she loved it.*

By the time he was done, her sex tingled. She was undeniably wet, the inside of her thighs slick with her arousal. Her clit felt swollen, throbbing, aching for a firmer, more intimate touch in order to claim the orgasm pulsing for a release. Never would she have believed being flogged would stimulate and

ERIKA WILDE

excite her to the brink of climax, yet that's exactly what had happened.

Holding her gaze, Black Heart pushed two fingers between her thighs and glided them along her pussy, careful not to tip her over that precarious edge she was teetering on. "You're drenched," he said, smiling triumphantly. "I think you're ready to be fucked."

She trembled all over at the thought of him giving her what she desperately needed. What she desperately wanted. *Oh, yes, please.*

He pulled on the chain that lowered her arms back down, and he unbuckled the soft leather cuffs, releasing her hands, then removed the scraps of her blouse still hanging from her shoulders. She fully expected him to take her over to the nearby couch, but instead he turned her around, slid his big hand up to the back of her neck, and pushed her upper body down until she was bent over a padded table, her cheek pressed to the cool leather. The edge of the bench was cushioned against her hips, and her breasts, still confined in the nipple clamps, rubbed enticingly against the surface.

THE CAPTURE

She instinctively tried to push her way back up, but he grabbed her hands and extended her arms above her head, then secured her wrists in the iron cuffs at the opposite end of the table. He hunched down behind her and spread her legs so he could wrap a length of chain around each of her ankles to shackle them to the opposite legs of the table, widening her stance and exposing her throbbing, needy pussy. She was still wearing her heeled boots, and she was grateful for the leather that provided protection from the rough metal links that would have rubbed harshly against her skin.

He straightened behind her and trailed his fingers down her spine, leaving shivers in his wake, despite her best efforts to suppress them. "Fucking perfect," he murmured appreciatively as he caressed a palm over her smooth, bare ass. "It doesn't get much more submissive than this, with you stretched out, spread open, and helpless to deny me anything I wish to do to you."

She turned her head to glance at him, galled by the man's smug confidence. "Do not mistake this for willingness or obedience,"

ERIKA WILDE

she snapped, refusing to yield in any way to her captor.

"Obedience, no," he agreed as one of his wicked fingers dipped along the crease of her buttocks and between her legs, sliding through the undeniable and slick evidence of her *willingness*. "But your body wants this. All this wet heat is *begging* for my cock to slam deep inside your tight pussy," he said as he dragged the tip of his finger over her hard, sensitive clit in a very pleasurable caress, teasing her with the promise of the release he kept just out of her reach. "Admit it."

*Yes, yes, yes!* Ignoring that brazen voice in her head, she closed her eyes and forced out a denial. "No. Never."

"Very well, then," he said, his tone more ruthless now as she heard him unbuttoning the front of his breeches. "Let's see just how *unwilling* you can be."

The naughty thrill of anticipation rushed through her, heightening her shameless need to be *taken* by this rogue pirate in an arousing display of forced seduction—exactly as she'd imagined, and written, in her fantasy. She gasped as he dragged the head of his cock along her slit from behind, using her moisture to lubricate himself, then pressed the engorged tip against the opening to her body, pressing in just a few delicious inches.

If she had the ability to push back into him, to entice him deeper, she would have done so. But the restraints around her wrists and ankles kept her immobile and him in complete control of the depth, pace, and level of sensual torment he planned to inflict upon her.

He leaned over her from behind, his hips aligning with hers, the heat of his chest blanketing her back. One of his hands twisted around her loose hair until he reached her scalp, and he pulled her head back until her throat was arched, thoroughly dominating her in every way.

His lips skimmed along her jaw up to the shell of her ear, his breathing already ragged and he'd yet to thrust the rest of the way inside her body. "I'm going to fuck you and make you mine," he said, his voice harsh and hot against her neck. "And since you refuse to admit that you want this, too, it's all for *my* pleasure, not yours. If you dare to come

ERIKA WILDE

while I'm inside of you, I will punish you all over again with the flogger, harder and longer, until you are too weak to even whimper. Do you understand?"

Her traitorous body quivered, and somehow, someway, she managed to utter a quiet, "Yes".

She curled her hands into fists against the iron shackles and braced herself for that first brutal, invading thrust. He didn't disappoint, plunging into her with a hard, long stroke that had her sucking in a startled breath and her inner walls clenching around his shaft. He was big and thick, stretching her, filling her, and with another jerk of his hips he seated himself even deeper still.

"Oh, fuck, yeah," he groaned in her ear as he withdrew from her body in a slow, tortuous drag of his rigid flesh against her sensitive inner tissues, before slamming home again with such force she was certain she'd have bruises across her hip area where she was bent over the table.

His free hand slid down between her legs, his index and middle finger gliding along the moist folds of her sex. He trapped her clit

THE CAPTURE

between those two digits, manipulating and pinching that bundle of nerves with just enough finesse to keep her teetering on the edge of an orgasm, yet not allowing her to free-fall over the edge. Her stomach tightened and rolled as the ache between her legs intensified, then ebbed when his fingers stopped plucking and stroking her flesh.

Her thighs shook, and she moaned in frustration, and she could have sworn she heard the rogue chuckle softly, wickedly, against her neck.

He flexed his hips, his thrusts slowing into a steady, rhythmic grind against her ass. His cock shuttled into her pussy and withdrew at a leisurely pace, her body feeling every heated inch of him as he slid all the way in, then gradually eased back out. Again and again and again . . .

Needy little noises welled up in her throat, and she tried to push back against him, to urge him harder, faster, deeper—she desperately needed the friction, inside and out—but she was anchored tight to the table and could barely squirm.

He nipped at her shoulder, then soothed

57

the sting of pain with a soft lap of his tongue. "I think I've made you suffer long enough, wench."

She nearly sobbed in relief at his words, but quickly realized when he removed his fingers from her clit, released her hair, and straightened behind her, that the end of her suffering did not mean he'd changed his mind about letting her climax. Oh, no, this was all about him finally seeking out his own release, and taking his own pleasure just as he'd claimed.

His broad hands gripped her hips, and he literally nailed her to the bench with the next rough thrust, as did the rapid succession of thrusts that followed. He groaned, his control vanishing as he slammed so far inside of her that she'd be lucky if she could still walk once he was done with her.

His body finally tensed and a hoarse cry of release echoed in the chamber as he emptied himself inside of her, then collapsed against her back once he was done.

Through it all, he never let her come.

## CHAPTER 5

*D*ean slid into the large copper tub behind the gorgeous, sexy woman he'd bought as his slave, the steaming water rising up to the edge as he added his muscular weight to the old-fashioned, claw-foot bathtub that had been built with plenty of comfort for two.

With a soft, blissful sigh, Jillian reclined against his chest and rested her head on his shoulder, her palms sliding along his legs that were straddling her from behind. She'd gathered her long hair into a loose, messy topknot to keep it from getting wet. The heat of the water, scented with a lemon almond bath oil, gave her complexion a rosy glow—or

ERIKA WILDE

maybe that sheen was a result of her being well and truly fucked, even if he hadn't allowed her to reach her own orgasm. Yet.

He would, in due time, he mused as he caressed his hands along her arms, her skin soft and slick from the water and fragrant oil. Their first scenario as pirate and wench had been all about punishing her for trying to escape, then her refusing to admit she wanted him. Her body had been undeniably wet and aroused, taking his cock with ease, but she'd played the part of stubborn damsel just as he knew she would so that he'd be provoked to force her into submission.

If there was one thing he'd learned about his wife and her sexual preferences over the past few months of their experimenting together, he'd come to discover that she liked it a little rough, along with a sting of pain, and she loved it when he exerted his strength and power over her, mentally and physically, when it came to fucking her. His dominate side loved it, too, that he had a wife who allowed him—encouraged him even—to embrace those darker desires he'd suppressed for most of their twenty year marriage.

THE CAPTURE

Now, the sexual games they played were almost always bolstered by elements of BDSM, and he definitely enjoyed surprising his wife with all the different ways they could add a bit of kink to their sex lives.

When he'd plucked one of her favorite fantasies that she'd written down and put into the glass vase in their playroom at home for them to draw inspiration from, he'd immediately known that his weekend get-a-way would be all about fulfilling that forbidden, provocative, and erotic adventure. The moment he'd made his presence known at the auction as the ruthless Black Heart, he'd seen the secret thrill in her eyes, and falling into character had been fun and hot as hell for him, too.

She rolled her head to the side and glanced up at him, her hazy eyes meeting his, rerouting his thoughts and attention back to her. "So, how is it that this tub was filled with steaming hot water just as we needed it?"

After their intense scene in the other room, he'd released her limbs from all the various restraints, then picked up her slack body in his arms and carried her to the bath-

61

ERIKA WILDE

room, where a bath had been prepared, just as he'd asked. Jillian had been delighted by the surprise, and he was glad that he'd had the foresight to make the request, especially since he'd been so aggressive with her. Undoubtedly, her body was feeling the effects of being taken so barbarically.

"I've discovered that the island of Eden is a very magical place," he said as he trailed the tips of his fingers across her stomach beneath the water. "I've set up a few things and let staff know what I wanted done, and approximately when, and so far, everything has fallen into place perfectly."

"I'm impressed, and this bath is so nice and relaxing after what you did to me in that dungeon room," she said with a smile. "My muscles were so tense, and soaking them feels so good."

He skimmed his hands up to her breasts, cupping the weight of both in his palms. He ran his thumbs over the tips, and didn't miss the slight catch of her breath. He'd taken the clamps off her nipples before she'd immersed herself in the tub, and he hoped he hadn't left them on for too long.

THE CAPTURE

"Are your nipples sore?" he asked, his voice reflecting his concern.

"They're a little tender," she said, and moaned softly when he very gently circled her areolas with a tip of a finger in a soothing touch. "But you're making them feel *much* better."

He chuckled and nuzzled his nose against her ear. "And the flogging? It wasn't too much?"

"It was perfect. As if you've been doing it for a while." She arched a brow, silently questioning his expertise and skills.

He revealed another surprise. "I had one of the Doms at The Players Club give me a few lessons on flogging, just to make sure I didn't hurt you in any way."

"I'd definitely let you do it again," she said, her voice dropping to a low, husky pitch as she rubbed her thighs together beneath the water, a telltale sign that she was still hot and bothered. "The whole fantasy, from the auction, to you capturing me when I escaped, to being flogged and fucked in the dungeon, was incredibly exciting and arousing. You made the scene feel very real, and other than

63

ERIKA WILDE

denying me an orgasm, I have no complaints."

Yeah, she was still a little miffed about him withholding her climax. "Maybe next time you won't be so stubborn and disobedient."

"Next time?" she asked hopefully.

"The fantasy isn't over yet, sweetheart," he assured her. "We've got tonight and all day tomorrow, and I'm not done pillaging and plundering the wench I paid a fortune for."

"Thank goodness," she said, the excitement back in her voice.

She turned around in the large tub to face him, almost sloshing water over the edge as she settled on her knees between his spread thighs. Her gorgeous tits were now out of the water, her nipples dripping with beads of moisture he wanted to lap off with his tongue. With a sultry smile, she cupped both of those luscious mounds in her hands, squeezing and fondling them, deliberately tempting him.

It worked. She lightly pinched her nipples, gasped, and gave him a coy look that sent a rush of heat straight to his cock.

THE CAPTURE

"Mayhap I can entice my new master to take care of this terrible, throbbing ache I have between my legs," she said, reverting back to character and reigniting her pirate fantasy while her hands traveled lower, dipping into the water and sliding straight down to her pussy. "Or mayhap, you'd rather watch me touch myself . . ."

She must have stroked across her sensitive clit, because she closed her eyes, dropped her head back, and let out a sweet moan that nearly convinced him to take his own cock in his fist and jerk-off to the erotic, dick-pulsing show. In a different scenario, he would have given an enthusiastic *hell yes*, but he'd held back her orgasm for a reason, to teach her a lesson as his *slave*, and there was no way he was going to allow her to give herself that ultimate pleasure by her own hand . . . or fingers, as it may be.

No, when that explosive orgasm happened, it was going to belong to *him*. Given by him. Taken by him. Her surrender savored by only him.

Recognizing those sexy noises she made in the back of her throat just before she came spurred him into action. He jolted forward so fast that this time water did splash over the rim, which also startled Jillian. Her eyes blinked open just as he plunged his hands beneath the surface and grasped her wrists, yanking them away from her body.

"I didn't give you permission to come, wench," he said, his voice dark with warning.

She bit her bottom lip, her expression etched with frustration. "I'm dying for an orgasm after what you put me through earlier. I'm so on edge, it hurts."

"That's exactly where I want you to be," he said, brushing his thumbs across the pulse points in her wrist. "I was serious when I said *I* would decide when it's time for you to come. If you dare to touch yourself again, I will lock you in a chastity belt and find my own pleasure in much more creative ways."

Her eyes widened at the threat, but she didn't provoke him further. She knew him well enough to realize that he wouldn't hesitate to follow through on his ultimatum.

She tossed her head back, her only display of rebellion. "The name Black Heart really does fit you."

THE CAPTURE

He smirked. "Aye, it does," he murmured. "I'm going to let you go, but I expect you to keep your hands and fingers to yourself, and off your pussy. Just relax, and I promise you'll be rewarded for your good behavior."

"Relax?" she repeated skeptically, an adorable pout on her lips. "Easy for you to say. You already *had* an orgasm."

He chuckled. "Yeah, and it was pretty fucking awesome, too."

She wrinkled her nose at him. "No one likes a braggart. Or a rogue."

"Oh, you *love* the rogue," he said all too knowingly. "And this particular rogue is *very* hungry."

He stood up, and pulled her to her feet at the same time. Water sluiced down their naked bodies, and he helped her out of the tub and onto a thick floor mat, then dried her off with a warm, fluffy towel. He slipped on one of the soft, luxurious robes hanging from a hook on the wall, and wrapped her up in the other one, then tied the sash. There was no sense in them getting dressed since he wasn't done having his way with her tonight.

Her stomach growled, and she gave him

ERIKA WILDE

an impish look. "I guess I'm hungry, too. I haven't eaten anything since breakfast."

"Then let's go eat dinner." Grabbing her hand, he led her out of the bathroom and gave her a quick, lascivious grin over his shoulder. "Though consider yourself warned, slave, because I plan to have *you* for dessert."

"I can't wait," she said, her voice breathless.

They stepped into the main room, and while they'd been enjoying their bath, someone had come into the cottage and set up the table with their evening meal. There were silver platters of food laid out, lit candles burning in crystal holders, and a bottle of Bollinger champagne resting on ice, just as he'd requested.

She glanced from the single place setting and lone champagne flute arranged at the end of the table, to him. "Does only one of us get to eat?" she asked curiously.

"No, we only need one setting because I'm going to feed you." He sat down on the chair and tugged her onto his lap.

She settled herself across his hard thighs and batted her lashes playfully at him. "Why,

Mr. Black Heart, are you trying to seduce me?"

"Pirates don't seduce," he replied gruffly, playing the part of a scoundrel and blackguard. "They abduct, demand, and ravage what's theirs. I believe I've already proven all three dark and dangerous qualities right beyond that red door, and I have no qualms doing it again."

She smiled and touched her fingers to his jaw. "I really don't think that heart of yours is as black as you claim."

Jillian had always seen the best in him, even when he, himself, had believed the worst. Even now, in a fantasy element, she was trying to soothe the savage beast who'd imprisoned her, but he maintained the pretense of a dominant pirate. "Do not mistake my kindness in feeding you for tenderness or leniency."

He glanced over at the buffet of food spread out before them—bites of lobster to dip in melted butter, grilled baby lamb chops with a creamy mint sauce, strips of orange beef tenderloin, and mini crab cakes—and picked up a succulent piece of lobster. He immersed it in the garlic butter sauce and fed it to her, letting his fingers rub enticingly over her lips before taking a bite for himself.

She moaned in pure delight as she chewed the succulent shellfish. "Oh my God, that is the best lobster I've ever had. I could get used to this."

He had to agree. So far, everything about the island of Eden was high quality, luxurious, and indulgent. From their accommodations, to their fantasy, to the feast that had been prepared for them to eat.

He also loved being able to spoil her, to give back to his wife for all those years she'd taken care of him, supporting him even through those more difficult times. He'd tried to do the same in his own alpha-male way and being the provider of the family, but now he was learning that it was the little things he did that meant so much to her, and made her feel special. Like something as simple as feeding her this meal.

THE CAPTURE

HE POURED a glass of expensive champagne, bringing the crystal rim to her mouth to let her take a drink of the sparkling wine. He continued to let her sample each of the dishes, using only his fingers as utensils, which made the process more sensual and decadent.

Once they were done with the main entries and had consumed nearly the entire bottle of Bollinger, he reached for one of the chocolate covered strawberries—one of her favorite confections—and lifted it to her lips.

"Dessert?" she asked oh-so-seductively.

"Yours, not mine," he assured her with a rakish grin. "I'll eat mine in just a bit."

Her lashes fell half-mast, and a seductive smile curved her mouth as she very provocatively licked the tip of the treat, making him imagine that sinful tongue lapping across the head of his cock, which was quickly stiffening against her ass. She slowly sank her teeth into the fruit, and gasped as the juices inside the strawberry spurted out, trickling down her chin and dripping onto her chest.

Startled by just how succulent the berry was, her eyes widened as she raised a hand to

ERIKA WILDE

catch the liquid splashing into the opening of her robe.

"Put your hands down," he ordered before she could stop the juices from dripping down her body. "I'll clean it up."

Obeying him, she lowered her arms and continued to chew the strawberry in her mouth, realization dawning in her eyes. "The fruit is infused with amaretto. No wonder there was so much juice inside. Between the champagne and the dessert, are you trying to get me drunk so you can take advantage of me?" she accused softly.

He laughed as he tugged on the sash of her robe, then spread the sides open, baring her naked body to his gaze. "Not drunk. I just want you to feel good."

She swiped her tongue lazily along her bottom lip, licking up the remnant flavors of strawberry and amaretto. "I already feel *very* good."

"It's about to get better." Cupping the back of her neck in one of his palms, he dipped his head to lick away the juice on her chin, then settled his mouth over hers in a deep, passionate, tongue-tangling kiss while his

THE CAPTURE

other hand rubbed the half-eaten strawberry and melting chocolate all over her breasts.

She moaned and shifted restlessly on his lap, her back arching as he coated her nipples in the sticky fruit and juice. Her fingers threaded through his hair, and she attempted to tug his head lower, obviously trying to pull his mouth down to her breasts.

He lifted his mouth from hers and aimed a dark look at her face. Sensual agony etched her features, and her eyes were glazed with lust and need. "Have you forgotten who's in charge, slave?" he demanded gruffly.

"No," she said, the harsh bite in his voice yanking her out of the sensual fog she'd slipped into. "You are, master."

"Then release my hair and do not try and dictate what you want me to do, nor will you come until I allow you to or else I will restrain your hands and legs again." He skimmed the ripe strawberry down her quivering stomach, circling it slowly, erotically, around her navel. "Do you understand?"

Her fingers untangled from his hair, and she sucked in a breath when he deliberately slid the fruit lower, rubbing the juices and

ERIKA WILDE

pulp across her bare mound. "I . . . I don't think I can hold back."

"You can. You *will*." He buried his face against the side of her neck, lapping away a trickle of nectar from her skin, then followed the trail down to breasts to lick them clean, too. "Now open your legs *wide*, wench."

She hesitated for a moment, then slowly parted her knees, opening herself to him. He smeared the sticky sweetness along the inside of her thighs, then dragged the juicy, amaretto infused strawberry along her slit, coating the folds of her sex with the lush dessert . . . again and again, while tracing an unhurried, maddening path around her clit.

"That's for me to enjoy later, when I feast on your cunt." He swirled his tongue around her nipple, his teeth nipping just hard enough to walk that fine line between pain and pleasure.

Jillian whimpered, unable to remember a time when her body had been strung so tautly, with her struggling not to give in to the need pulsing between her legs. Her head fell back and with every slick pass of the fruit along her pussy, her breathing deepened and

THE CAPTURE

her hips undulated of their own accord, until she feared there was no stopping the orgasm gathering like a violent storm within her, just seconds from unleashing its fury—despite any consequences she'd have to endure from her rogue pirate.

The delicious swell of ecstasy started to crest, then abruptly eased off when he pulled his mouth from her nipple and no longer stroked her with the strawberry.

"Such a good girl," he praised with a satisfied smile. "Are you finally ready to submit to me?"

She drew in a shuddering breath and nodded. In the dungeon room, she'd been all about being stubborn and rebellious, and she'd paid the price for her defiance. Now, she was willing to give him anything he wanted from her, so long as it resulted in her own pleasure.

"Get on your knees in front of me," he commanded. "Take off your robe and unclip your hair so I can wrap those silky strands around my fist while I fuck your mouth."

Heat and desire collided in her belly at his raw words, and she didn't hesitate to do his

ERIKA WILDE

bidding. Moving off his lap, she shrugged out of her robe, released her hair from the top-knot on her head so that the thick strands tumbled around her shoulders, then knelt in front of him, anxiously awaiting his next order.

He offered her a pleased smile for her obedience as he tugged open his own robe with one hand, while the other still held the half-eaten strawberry. The lapels of the robe fell to the sides, and her gaze traveled from his toned, muscular chest, along his ripped belly, all the way down to the hard, thick column of flesh jutting up from between his spread legs. A large bead of pre-come formed on the engorged crest, and her mouth watered for a taste of him in the worst way.

He wrapped his fingers around the base of his cock, holding it upright, and she watched in fascination and sexual hunger as he smeared the strawberry-amaretto nectar up and down his erection, until his shaft was coated with the dessert. He brought the macerated fruit to the head of his penis and swiped it over the bead of moisture leaking from the tip, then reached out and rubbed

THE CAPTURE

the sticky sweetness of all their combined juices along her bottom lip.

"Eat it," he said, and pushed what was left of the berry and melting chocolate into her mouth.

She chewed, undeniably aroused by all the decadent flavors passing over her tongue, both sweet and salty. His essence and hers, all wrapped up in a candied confection.

She licked her lips with a sultry swipe of her tongue and glanced up at him, where he was reclining in the chair like a king—a gorgeous, magnificently naked sultan, presiding over his submissive concubine. "I want more."

"Don't worry, there's plenty more for you to enjoy right here," he said, his husky voice tinged with amusement. "You have a mess to clean up, slave, so get to work."

Dying to have him in her mouth, she moved between his thighs and wrapped her fingers around the hot width of his shaft, then licked her way from the base of his erection all the way to the burgeoning head, slowly, leisurely, again and again, taking her time to savor every bit of her dessert—and

ERIKA WILDE

torment *him* in the process this time around.

Another swirl of her tongue around the crown, and he made an inarticulate, impatient sound in the back of his throat that told her time for play was over. He wound her hair around his fist until his fingers reached her scalp and there was no way she could escape his hold as he ruthlessly pushed his way past her lips and fed her his cock, until the head of his dick bumped and rubbed against the back of her throat.

She moaned the same time as he did, the sound vibrating along his shaft as he guided her head back up the length of him. She sucked at him until her cheeks hallowed, her lips sealing tight around him so that he felt every retreating inch.

"So fucking good," he rasped as he continued to fuck her mouth, thrusting deep, withdrawing then plunging back in again.

She glanced up at him, and the intense pleasure spreading across the hard angles of his face spurred her on. The power she held over him, even temporarily, made her soar and ramped up her own arousal. She was

THE CAPTURE

swollen and drenched between her thighs, her need to be touched and stroked an excruciating ache.

Abruptly, he cursed and pulled her mouth off of him, his breathing ragged as if he was grasping at his own thin threads of control—which gratified her, considering she'd been in that condition for most of the afternoon.

She blinked oh-so-innocently at him. "Did I do something wrong?"

He smirked at her. "No, I'm just thinking it's *almost* time to let you come."

With that announcement, he stood up, and helped her to her feet, too. He walked over to the bed and laid down in the middle, his head propped on a pillow, and crooked his finger at her.

"Come here and straddle my face, slave," he said boldly. "I want to eat my dessert off your thighs and pussy while you suck my cock."

His request was unmistakable, and the muscles in Jillian's belly clenched at the thought of engaging in the simultaneous oral sex position with him, which would result in a guaranteed orgasm for her—*finally*!

ERIKA WILDE

Much too anxiously, she climbed up on the mattress and arranged her knees on either side of his head, spreading her legs so that she was completely open to him and his gaze, his mouth, his hands. She lowered her body over the top of his, her belly gliding across his chest and her breasts rubbing against the light furring of hair on his abdomen as she settled into the erotic 69 position.

Her pirate's hard-as steel cock stood up in greeting, and while she could feel his damp breath feathering along her inner thigh, he waited for her to slide her lips over him before he did anything on his end. The stroke of her tongue produced a long, hot lick from him, followed by nibbling bites all the way up to her core that teased her with the promise of what she wanted so damned badly.

Closing her eyes, she sucked him deep, and he spread open her folds and raked his tongue through her clit. She moaned, swallowing around the head of his cock that was lodged against the back of her throat, and he rewarded her with a slow, swirling lick around her clit that made her legs quiver.

THE CAPTURE

"Umm, you taste so fucking good," he breathed against her as he pulled the hard, sensitive nub into his mouth and gently raked it with his teeth.

The shocking sensation was like a live wire, touching off the nerves in her pussy and triggering the beginnings of a fierce orgasm she knew she'd never be able to contain. With a soft cry she released his cock and tossed her head back, on the verge of embracing an earth-shattering climax.

A sharp, jarring slap to her ass jolted her senses, immediately diffusing the orgasm in lieu of her brain focusing on the unexpected sting of pain. It was as though her mind and body were torn in two different directions, and pleasure was not the priority when her flesh burned from her rogue's wicked form of discipline.

"Greedy wench," he growled against her thigh, and she could have sworn she felt him smile. "You don't come until I do."

"Bastard," she said out of pure, disgruntled annoyance that he once again held all the power.

He chuckled and flicked his tongue

ERIKA WILDE

against her sensitive clit. "Aye, I am. You'll get your orgasm when I get mine."

She was fully prepared to work for it, to pull out her own special feminine tricks to speed up the process for him, too. She gripped him in a tight fist and cupped his sacs in her other hand, going down on his cock while fondling his balls and occasionally rubbing a damp finger along that erogenous zone along his perineum.

She knew she hit the spot when his thighs and abdomen tensed and he increased his efforts on his end, adding the thrust of two fingers deep inside her body while his tongue circled and swirled and drove her right back up to that precipice. Her body undulated with the rhythm of his fingers, shamelessly riding his mouth as her lips and throat worked his throbbing cock, squeezing him, milking him, until he was forced to let go and give himself over to her.

Groaning, he anchored an arm around her bucking hips, holding her tight to his open mouth and marauding tongue as she flew apart at the same exact moment he did. A release of gigantic proportions wracked

THE CAPTURE

her entire being, the ecstasy so intense she wanted to scream, but couldn't.

She could only moan around his pulsing shaft as she swallowed everything he had to give, and he did the same as they both succumbed to pure unadulterated bliss.

## CHAPTER 6

"Wake up sleeping beauty."

Her rogue woke her up the same way he'd exhausted her last night . . . with his mouth between her legs and his tongue doing deliciously wicked things to her flesh. He licked and swirled, slow and lazy, murmuring encouragements as he let the sensations build—and not denying her a thing when her orgasm rolled through her like a luxurious wave.

This time, when she gripped his hair to press him closer, he let her.

This time, she was able to scream her pleasure as her body convulsed with shimmering ecstasy.

THE CAPTURE

It was a delightful way to start the day, and as the sensations gradually ebbed, he moved up over her body so that they were face to face. He rested his upper body on his forearms to keep his weight from squashing her, while his hips settled between her spread thighs, the heated glide of his erection nestling against her entrance.

"Morning, baby girl," he murmured affectionately, his gray eyes smoky with his own unfulfilled desire.

She smiled at the endearment he used, realizing she wasn't waking up to her dominant pirate, but her husband who wanted a lazy, satisfying morning in bed. It had been a while since they'd indulged in plain 'ol vanilla missionary sex, for the sole purpose of making love, and it was a lovely change of pace from the intensity of yesterday.

"Morning," she greeted him as she stroked her fingers down the slope of his toned, muscular back. "That was nice, though after last night's crazy, wild, intense orgasm, I wasn't sure I'd *ever* have another in me," she teased.

He chuckled softly and nuzzled her jaw,

all the way up to her ear. "Then let's go for two in a row," he said, and with a flex of his hips he filled her up, then started moving inside her.

She arched beneath him and exhaled on a low moan of pleasure, the unrushed, luxurious slide of him stoking that slow burn of need she knew would eventually catch fire in the most tantalizing way.

He reached down with a hand, hooked his fingers behind one of her knees, and pulled her leg up so it draped around his waist. "Wrap that other gorgeous leg around me so I can get as deep as possible," he said, his voice a sexy, husky rasp.

She did, hooking her ankles together at the base of his spine, loving how it locked their bodies together so intimately. The position tilted her hips up and aligned them in a way that allowed him the hottest, deepest penetration possible and made her acutely aware of the ridges in his cock dragging against the sensitive bundle of nerves inside of her.

He groaned and lowered his mouth to hers, her own lips automatically parting to accept the sweep of his tongue as he deepened the kiss.

With each long, measured pump of his hips, he gyrated against her clit, giving her the friction she craved that reignited a tingling, enticing anticipation. She could feel the passion in him escalate, could taste his rising hunger as he seduced her mouth with his, and claimed her with his hard, strong body.

He lifted his mouth from hers and stared down at her, their gazes locked, his eyes dark with desire, the rhythm of his thrusts increasing as he drove into her harder, stronger, faster. She recognized that unraveling of his self-discipline, and knew he was close to finding his release. His breathing turned choppy, and with a low growl of pleasure he tossed his head back and arched high and hard, letting go of his restraint as he pumped erratically into her, his cock pulsing hot and deep.

Jillian's body clenched around his shaft, the knot of desire within her tightening. Her husband was a man who prided himself on his control, in all things, and watching him completely let go and give himself over to her, physically and emotionally, never failed to increase her pleasure . . . especially when he looked back down at her, his jaw clenching, and demanded in a sexy, husky rasp, "give me what I want, Jillian."

Her alpha, take-charge husband was back. She shuddered as he continued to grind against her, giving her everything she needed to push her right over and into her own heady climax. A soft cry escaped her, and she writhed beneath him, rocking her hips up against his while her body convulsed in a languid, sublime orgasm.

With a groan, he collapsed on top of her, giving them both time to come back to their senses before he rolled off, then gathered her close to his side. He covered her with the sheet, and she snuggled against his chest, feeling relaxed and content.

She hadn't realized just how much she and Dean had needed the time away from their jobs and hectic daily life, to reconnect and rejuvenate that spark between them all over again. It wasn't so much about the pirate fantasy he'd created, but rather just the two

THE CAPTURE

of them enjoying their time together, stress-free.

She laid in his arms for a while, feeling no pressure to have to get up and get started on the day—the beauty of being on a vacation. The time was theirs, to do as they pleased, to enjoy whatever they wanted to do at their own pace. They still had one more day left on Eden, and she was curious to know what, if anything, Dean had planned.

She glanced up at him, the hand on his chest tracing lazy patterns up and down his abdomen. "So, what are we doing today?"

He smiled at her. "I thought we could explore the island, then tonight you have a date with Black Heart," he said, waggling his brows at her in a very lascivious way.

She was thrilled to hear that she'd be spending more time with her rogue pirate. "Where are we going on this date?"

"I'm not spoiling the surprise." His gaze took on a very wicked glint. "But I can guarantee the evening will be fun, naughty, and probably *very* kinky."

"Sounds perfect," she said, already anticipating the evening's wild and salacious activities.

AFTER EATING a light breakfast and showering, Jillian found a few items hanging in the armoire for her to wear. She selected the plain pale blue sundress in a lightweight cotton, then searched for a pair of panties . . . and couldn't find any.

Frowning, she glanced over her shoulder at Dean, who'd put on a pair of dark brown casual linen drawstring pants that he'd cuffed up to his calves. "What is it about this place and undergarments, or lack thereof?" she asked in exasperation.

"That was based on my request," he said with an unapologetic shrug. "I like the thought of you being completely naked beneath your clothes."

She raised a brow and dropped her gaze to the crotch of his pants and the unmistakable outline of his cock. "Well, at least you're going commando, too."

He chuckled. "Absolutely." He put on a

THE CAPTURE

pair of men's flip-flops, and she slipped into some sandals. "Now let's go and see what the island has to offer."

They headed out of the cottage, and Dean grabbed her hand and guided her down a dirt path filled with lush foliage and tropical flowers. Exotic birds flew overhead, and Jillian was enchanted by all the gorgeous butterflies and hummingbirds fluttering about. The landscape was stunning, providing a visual treat everywhere they looked, and definitely earned the island the name of Eden.

After a while, she heard the sound of rushing water, and the trail they were following finally ended at a lagoon with water so clear and blue it almost looked unreal. At the far end was a huge rock formation with a cascading waterfall. The day was warm and humid, and she had to admit that the spray from the down rush of water on her skin felt good and inviting.

A quick glance around told her that the area was secluded and private. A clearing to the left had been set up with a blanket spread out on the ground in a spot dappled by sunlight, and a picnic basket awaited them for lunch. Behind that scene was a canvas hammock tied between two trees.

She didn't have to ask Dean to know that he'd arranged this adventure, and she silently gave him kudos for being so creative and romantic.

"Ready to go skinny dipping?" he asked.

"Are you sure we'll be alone?" The last thing she wanted was to get caught in the buff by a stranger who happened to stroll by.

"Guaranteed," he assured her with a wink. "This is our private lagoon for the afternoon. You game to get naked?"

She nodded eagerly. "Oh, yeah." Swimming in the nude was something she'd always wanted to do, but there had never been a good time or place . . . until now.

She pulled off her dress, and in this instance she was grateful that she wasn't wearing any underwear beneath. Dean shucked his pants, and she ran into the lagoon ahead of him, sucking in a quick breath as the cold water shocked her warm skin and entire system. She came to an abrupt stop hip deep, while Dean dove

THE CAPTURE

straight into the pool and surfaced a few feet away from her. Seeing that she'd yet to fully submerse herself, he grinned wickedly and splashed her unmercifully.

She squealed like a young girl while trying unsuccessfully to ward off the avalanche of water he sent her way. Once she was drenched she retaliated, and a battle of waterworks ensued between them, until they were both laughing and dripping wet.

For the next hour they swam and played, chasing one another and letting the capture end in steamy kisses and slow, slick caresses. They made out like teenagers beneath the waterfall, and while the desire between them simmered on a slow burn, neither one of them felt the frantic need to slake their lust. Between this morning's love making, and tonight's promise of something wild and erotic, this lazy afternoon was all about enjoying the build of sexual tension, knowing that this evening would bring pleasure and satisfaction.

They ate a picnic lunch of finger sandwiches and fruit, drank a bottle of wine, and took a nap together in the hammock. The swaying motion of the canvas bed lulled them both to sleep while Jillian cuddled close to Dean's chest, his arm draped around her.

When they returned to the cottage hours later, and she came out of the bathroom from taking a hot shower, a new outfit had been laid out on the bed for her to wear for tonight's outing. While Dean disappeared into the dungeon room to get dressed himself, Jillian put on her costume—a white, button-up shirtdress that ended above the knee in a soft cascade of feminine ruffles, and a black and purple leather vest that cinched up tight through her waist and bust and plumped together her unbound breasts. Instead of knee-high boots, she'd been provided with a pair of black patent leather, four inch stilettos.

She glanced into the mirror inside the armoire, feeling incredibly sexy and daring. She'd curled her hair and left it down, and her skin glowed pink from the kiss of sun during today's outing at the lagoon. She smiled at her reflection, at how provocative and seductive she looked, and how that

THE CAPTURE

confidence made her body buzz with awareness.

"Jesus," Dean grated out from behind her. "You look hot enough to fuck."

She spun around, giving him a sassy smile. "I believe that's the goal tonight, isn't it?"

"Oh, hell yeah," he murmured huskily, his heated gaze raking down the length of her, then back up again.

He'd changed into his pirate attire of black breeches, white shirt, and waistcoat, and a long sword was attached to his leather belt. He strolled toward Jillian, and her gaze dropped to the strip of black leather and length of chain he held in his hand.

A frisson of excitement coursed through her, making her feel breathless. "What's that for?"

He lifted up the leather collar and the chain leash attached to it, a very Black Heart smirk curving his lips. "You're still my captive and my slave, and tonight you'll be treated as such."

Moving behind her, he wrapped the soft, fur-lined collar around her throat, pushed

ERIKA WILDE

her hair to one side, and securely buckled the two inch wide strap behind her neck before coming to stand in front of her again. The chain leash connected to a silver ring in front, and he gave it a slight tug on the snug collar that accelerated her pulse—in a very arousing way.

"This is to keep you in line and to make sure every man in the room knows you're mine," he said, his entire demeanor taking on that dangerous edge of an unscrupulous pirate. "I will not tolerate your disobedience tonight, in any way, do you understand?"

In this fantasy element, his authority thrilled her, and she nodded, prepared to be the *willing* wench he wanted. Tonight wasn't about struggling and denying herself, it was about enjoying and savoring the pleasure of being this man's obedient slave.

"Yes, master," she said softly.

He gave her a pleased smile, gave a gentle tug on the leash that propelled her forward, and headed for the door. "Let's go and have some fun."

## CHAPTER 7

They arrived back to the scene where the auction had taken place the day before, but the inside of the tavern had been transformed into what looked and felt like an open-area brothel. The auction dais was still present, but the place was more dimly lit with candles on the tables and sconces on the walls. Pirates and sailors were chasing laughing harlots, and others had succumbed to more pleasurable pursuits right there in the spacious room filled with upholstered lounge chairs and settees.

She followed her master through the establishment, taking it all in with wide, fascinated eyes. The pirate atmosphere remained, but there was no mistaking that this evening's fantasy was an old-time version of what transpired at the more modern day Players Club. Tonight was all about sexual satisfaction, erotic scenarios, and watching and enjoying hedonistic desires being played out.

They walked past a couple who were in the throes of fucking—the young sailor had the curvy woman bent over a table, her voluminous skirts shoved around her waist while he took her from behind. Another woman was deep-throating a man's cock while another stood behind her with a soft leather whip and smacked her pinkening ass with it while she moaned and sucked even harder. The sights and sounds aroused Jillian, made her skin flush and her pulse pound with her own rising lust.

Keeping a tight grip on the leash, Black Heart led her toward a vacant settee, and Jillian exhaled on a sharp, startled scream as a strong arm snagged her around the waist and she was pulled back against a hard, unyielding body. The attack was so unex-

THE CAPTURE

pected, she immediately struggled against the other man's hold.

Black Heart spun around, fast and lithe, drawing the sword at his waist with precision and ease as he pointed the sharp-edged tip at the adversary behind her. "Let her go, Howell," he demanded in a low, menacing tone of voice. "And I *may* let you live."

*Howell*, the man who'd bid against Black Heart to win her as his slave, tightened his arm around her, his face much too close to hers as he dared to caress the tips of his fingers along the exposed curve of her breast. "And what if she prefers another master to the likes of you?" he asked snidely, challenging Black Heart.

"She is mine," he replied very calmly, though his gray eyes blazed with fury. "I will fight to the death for her. *Your* death."

"We shall see about that." With a hard push, Howell shoved Jillian out of the way and withdrew his own lethal looking sword.

She stumbled on her feet, and Black Heart let go of the lead connecting to her collar so she was out of harm's way and he could face-off with his rival. Jillian stood by the sidelines

ERIKA WILDE

with the rest of the crowd that had gathered, her heart racing in panic. She knew this had to be a prearranged act, but it all felt so very real, especially when Howell charged at Black Heart, his sword pointed directly at his chest.

Jillian gasped, but Black Heart was quick to deflect the attack and advance upon the other man, setting off a battle of strength and determination between the two men. The sound of steel clashing echoed in Jillian's ears as they engaged in combat and terror gripped her. Howell was a worthy opponent, but with every slash of the heavy sword, she could see the muscles in Black Heart's arm flex, until he eventually wore down the other man and over-powered him.

With a hard, swift, upswing, Black Heart dislodge the sword from Howell's grasp, sending it scattering across the floor. Without a weapon, the other man stumbled back, tripping on his own feet and falling flat on his ass. His eyes grew wide with fear as Black Heart advanced upon him, until he stood over his sprawled form, intimidating and formidable, and pressed the tip of his blade against Howell's heart.

THE CAPTURE

"Do you know why they call me Black Heart?" he asked the man he'd pinned beneath his sword. When Howell shook his head nervously, her pirate rogue grinned treacherously. "Because I carve out the hearts of the men who try and steal what's mine."

Howell swallowed hard, and knowing he'd lost this fight, his gaze turned pleading. "Spare me, please."

Black Heart considered his request, and glanced over at Jillian, giving her the choice as to the other man's fate.

She was so caught up in the realism of the performance, she blurted out, "Let him live," before Black Heart changed his mind.

"He doesn't deserve your mercy, but very well," he said, and motioned for two very burly sailors to come forward. "Howell will live, but not pleasantly. Take him away to the rat infested prisons below."

"Aye, as you wish," one of the sailors said, as the two of them restrained Howell and escorted him out of the tavern.

Jillian's knees went weak with relief that bloodshed had been avoided. But she had to admit, act or not, it had been exciting and

101

ERIKA WILDE

thrilling to watch Black Heart defend her honor and wield that sword with such expertise.

Black Heart sheathed his sword and strolled back toward Jillian, and the rest of the on-lookers broke out in cheers over his win. She watched her pirate approach, her breath catching in her throat at his sexy swagger and the triumphant gleam in his eyes. Reaching her, he circled an arm around her waist and brought her body flush to his.

"Is this the part where I swoon?" she couldn't resist asking playfully. "Because that sword fight was *definitely* swoon-worthy."

He chuckled in amusement, but there was a seriousness in the depths of his gray eyes. "I will *always* protect you and what's mine."

Not just in this fantasy he'd created, but *always*. "I know," she whispered, then he celebrated his victory by claiming her mouth in a hot, tongue-tangling kiss she returned with just as much passion and ardor.

"Let the festivities resume!" someone in the tavern yelled, and another round of cheers went up from the revelers. "The sweetest, finest rum for the winner!"

THE CAPTURE

They returned to a vacant settee in a more secluded area of the brothel, where her pirate sat close beside her on the cushioned seat, his hand wrapped once again around the chain leash. A young, pretty girl delivered a ceramic stein of rum, her ample breasts nearly spilling from her low-cut bodice as she deliberately bent over to place it on the side table.

"This one's on the house," she said, batting her lashes at him. "And if there's anything else you want or need, just let me know. My name's Nicola."

The invitation in her voice was unmistakable, but Black Heart merely gave her a slow, lazy grin as he stroked a hand up Jillian's bare leg. "I already have everything I want or need right here."

With a disappointed pout, the woman moved on, quickly catching the eye of two men across the room who were more than willing to accommodate her. Nicola sat between the two sailors and started making out with one of them, while the other guy moved in close and began kissing her neck as his hand disappeared beneath her skirt.

ERIKA WILDE

Jillian had no idea if Nicola was a part of Black Heart's scenario, or if the other woman was possibly re-enacting a fantasy of her own. Either way, it was all consensual, all extremely erotic, and it set the tone for a very risqué evening.

Other salacious activities were starting to take place again, and Jillian realized that they had the best view in the place to watch all the debauchery unfolding in front of them, to be a voyeur to all the kinky display of sexual indulgences. Her blood rushed warm and languid through her veins, and she shifted restlessly, rubbing her legs together and finding that she was already wet and aroused.

"Sit on my lap, slave," Black Heart said, his gruff voice reflecting shades of his own lust at the various scenes going on around them.

She stood up, then started to sit sideways across his thighs, but he quickly redirected her. He grabbed her hips and settled her on his lap so that her back was pressed against his.

"I want you to face forward," he said, pulling on her skirt and arranging the mate-rial out of the way so that her bare bottom

THE CAPTURE

slid against the fabric of his breeches and the firm, solid press of his erection rubbed against her ass. "I want to make sure you see everything."

Oh, she could see everything, and every-one . . . and she realized that anyone glancing their way could see her, too. Her heart raced a bit faster at the thought. There was only a candle on the table beside them, but it was enough to cast a soft, hazy illumination, and she was grateful for the dim lighting that would at least provide a small measure of privacy.

"Look at Nicola and those two men," her pirate rogue whispered, his breath hot on her neck as he let go of her leash for a moment so that he could untie the strips of leather holding the front of her vest closed.

Jillian redirected her gaze back to the trio, her belly clenching at the sight of how Nico-la's position now reflected hers . . . the other woman was sitting on one of the sailor's thighs, facing forward, while the man sitting next to them was loosening her blouse. Once the ribbons on Nicola's corset fell away, the man behind her lifted her bare breasts in his

ERIKA WILDE

palms, offering a nipple to his partner, who eagerly took the hard nub in his mouth and sucked.

Nicola cried out, and Jillian shuddered, shocked to realize that while she'd been staring in a haze of desire at the trio, her own rogue had opened her top, slipped his hands inside, and had her breasts cupped in his hands. Startled, she covered his hands with her own, not sure she wanted herself on display.

"Let go," he murmured huskily, coaxing her to obey his command. "You have gorgeous breasts and I want to be able to see them, and touch them, and let every other man envy what is mine."

She was torn between saying no, and giving him what he wanted. It wasn't as though her breasts were young, small, and perky, like Nicola's. No, they were a woman's breasts—full and heavy, overflowing even in her pirate's large hands.

She closed her eyes, skewing up her courage to be so bold and brazen, which was more difficult than she'd imagined. Yet the more self-assured woman she'd become over

THE CAPTURE

the months pushed through, giving her the fortitude she needed to be so fearless. Everyone in this place was a stranger, and knowing she'd never see any of them ever again allowed her to shed those inhibitions in ways she never had before in a public setting.

Exhaling a breath, she let her hands fall away to her sides and opened her eyes once again, owning her sexuality, and focusing on the one and only thing that mattered . . . that her pirate thought she had gorgeous breasts. That knowledge alone made her feel powerful and sexy and confident.

"Good girl," he praised, openly rolling her nipples between his fingers, elongating them into stiff points before lifting her breasts higher, toward her mouth. "Lick them. Suck them. See how good you taste."

Oh, he was pushing all kinds of boundaries tonight, and now that Jillian had made the decision to embrace a more daring side, she refused to back down. She dragged her own tongue across the sensitive crest, pulled the tip deeper into her mouth, and moaned, her mind and body unprepared for the zing

ERIKA WILDE

of pleasure that arced straight down to her sex.

"Look at that man over there," Black Heart rasped in her ear. "The way he's watching you pleasure yourself, the way he's lusting for *you* even while another woman sucks his cock."

Her face flushed at the realization that someone had witnessed such a provocative act, but she glanced across the room, curious to see who this man was. To the right of the threesome, a well-garbed man, much like a ship captain, was sitting in a chair. His hands twisted tight in a woman's long hair while he pumped his shaft slow and steady into her mouth, his dark, hooded gaze locked on Jillian.

A secret thrill fluttered through her, catching her off guard.

"Ahh, you like being an exhibitionist." Black Heart's knowing voice cascaded along the side of her neck, and before she could refute his claim, he said, "Let's give him a show."

Her pirate brought her palms up to her own breasts so she could continue fondling

THE CAPTURE

them, while he pushed his hands between them and unfastened the front of his breeches. He shifted, freeing his erection, and she moaned as she felt the silken heat and length of his cock pressing insistently along the base of her spine. Plucking at her stiff nipples, and uncaring who watched, she wriggled her ass against him, suddenly desperate to feel him deep inside.

He secured an arm around her waist, lifting her up a few inches and positioning his shaft at her entrance before letting her slide back down, her body enveloping him in its slick heat until he was seated to the hilt. In this position, she felt him everywhere, his cock stretching her wide with a delicious burn.

She sighed blissfully, and he shuddered and groaned, long and low.

While she'd gotten used to her blouse being open and her breasts being exposed, she was grateful for the skirt he left draped around her thighs that gave her some modicum of modesty, even when he pushed his boots along the inside of her high heels and used his feet to spread her legs inde-

ERIKA WILDE

cently wide apart. The material of her skirt fell between her open thighs, shielding the most intimate part of her from anyone's gaze.

"Your pussy is mine, and mine alone," he said possessively, shifting once again behind her as his free hand searched for something in the pocket of his waistcoat. "That's one part of you that will never be shared with prying eyes. Ever."

Like the *captains*, she thought, shifting her gaze back to the man across the room, who hadn't looked away from her. He licked his lips, his jaw clenching as he forced his cock deeper into the woman's mouth. The wench swallowed every inch, her own hand pressed between her spread thighs as she worked herself to her own orgasm.

Jillian moaned softly from all the erotic visual stimulation. She squeezed her breasts and nipples as her gaze drifted to the three-some once again, an undeniable ache blooming deep in her womb upon seeing their new position. The sailor who'd been sitting by Nicola's side was now kneeling on the floor in front of her, his large hands pressed against the inside of her knees to

THE CAPTURE

keep her thighs spread wide open as he buried his mouth between her legs, and his partner fucked her from behind, exactly the way Jillian's own pirate was doing to her.

Jillian felt a hand slip beneath her skirt, and her entire body jolted when something soft and nubby fluttered against her pussy. She gasped and squirmed, trying to close her legs against the pulsating sensation, but unable to do so since her pirate had secured her feet wide apart.

"What . . . what is that?" she managed to ask.

"It's a finger vibrator," he said wickedly as he stroked it along the soft outer folds of her sex, titillating her sensitive flesh with the low, humming device. "I put it in my waistcoat pocket when I was in the dungeon room changing. Feels good, doesn't it? Like a tongue flicking along your pussy."

It felt *exactly* as he described . . . and reflected exactly what was happening to Nicola. Jillian watched, enthralled and unbearably aroused, as the man's head moved up and down between the other woman's thighs, licking her, sucking her, while the

ERIKA WILDE

man behind Nicola grasped her waist and thrust into her from his seated position, his face etched with carnal lust.

Black Heart mimicked the surge of his hips in rhythm to the man pumping into Nicola, filling Jillian again and again. He used the slim finger vibrator to replicate the threesome she was watching, making it *feel* as though she, too, had a hot mouth between her thighs and two men were pleasuring her at once.

With his free hand, Black Heart tightened his hand around the chain leash, until he reached her collar and was able to pull her head back to his shoulder and his mouth grazed her cheek. "Do you like what you see, and what you feel?" he asked, his voice dark and demanding as he drew slow circles around her swollen, needy clit with that wicked, fluttering device.

"Yes," she said, unable to lie. The entire scenario was so erotic, she just knew she was going to combust into a million pieces as soon as her pirate allowed her to. "But this threesome isn't a fantasy of mine," she added, wanting to be sure he realized that she didn't

THE CAPTURE

want or need another man that way. In any way at all.

"I know," he said, his teeth scraping enticingly along her jaw. "It's a fantasy of *mine*. You know it makes me hot when I think about another man lusting over you, fucking you, but in reality, I'd goddamn kill any guy who dared to touch you that way."

Oh, yes, she knew how much that particular fantasy inflamed him. She remembered the evening she'd taken him to a night club, when she'd danced with another man . . . and the aggressive, explosive sex they'd had afterward. The mind-blowing recollection ramped up the heat and need pouring through her, made her inner walls clench around his cock as the inklings of an orgasm began simmering low in her belly, deep in her core.

Nicola's cries of pleasure rang out, and Jillian glanced back at the woman in the throes of passion, the way she twisted her fingers in the man's hair who was going down on her, eating her, and pressing his mouth harder against her pussy. The man behind her increased his thrusts, and Nicola's hips began their own sensual dance as she gyrated against the cock inside her and the tongue flicking against her cunt. The man fucking her came on a hoarse shout, and she came on a raw scream, pure ecstasy etching her features.

Nicola's wanton response was like a spark to Jillian's fuse, and her climax swelled inside of her. She closed her eyes, letting her head fall back on her pirate's shoulder as she pushed her hips back into his driving, upward strokes, and let the fluttering licks on her clit send her over that same rapturous edge.

She felt a strong male hand curl around her neck, right above the collar, and guide her head back up.

"Open your eyes, slave," her rogue commanded against her ear. "Look. At. Him . . . *Now*."

So many sensations rioted within Jillian, but she forced her lashes to open, and found herself staring at the other man sitting in the chair across the room, who was staring at *her* with dark, hungry eyes. His expression tightened, his face flushed, and his lips parted on

THE CAPTURE

what looked like a groan. He gripped the woman's hair tighter and pumped harder, deeper, into her mouth, giving her no choice but to take all of him as he came.

Everything about tonight's experience was wild, crazy, and shameless, and witnessing a stranger's lust for her added more fuel to the fire burning inside of Jillian. Her mind and body felt battered with sensations, and with her rogue pirate driving deep into her channel, his hot, panting breath on her neck, she felt utterly possessed. Inside and out.

Like nothing she'd ever felt before.

She heard a long, ragged groan spill from her rogue's chest, knew that he'd reached his own climax, and followed him over. There was no way to hold back the tremendous orgasm that wracked its way through her, bowing her body with the strength and force of its fury, and wringing an unbridled scream from her lips as she rode out the intensity of her release.

She felt as though she'd blacked out, and when she finally came to her senses, everything and everyone around her seemed to

ERIKA WILDE

fade away in the aftermath. It was the man behind her who'd wrapped her safe and secure in her arms, *her husband*, who grounded her, and became her anchor.

He was her reality, and the only man who would ever claim her heart, her body, and her soul.

She lay limp and sated against him, and she reached up and touched his jaw. He lowered his head, skimming his lips along her cheek, and she heard him say the only words that mattered to her at all.

*I love you, baby girl.*

## CHAPTER 8

*D*ean glanced over at his wife, who was sitting in the plush leather seat next to his in the corporate jet he'd used to fly to Miami, before heading to Eden a few days ago in a small seaplane. Now, he and Jillian were heading back home to San Diego in the private aircraft, instead of taking a commercial flight, their time on the magical island over.

And it had definitely been magical, enchanting even. Everything about the place had met or exceeded his expectations, in so many ways. He'd planned the pirate fantasy, but Eden had brought it to life, had given it an authentic feel he couldn't have replicated anywhere else.

There were aspects of their weekend getaway that he knew Jillian had loved and enjoyed, but he still wasn't sure how she felt about what had transpired last night. Once they'd returned to their cottage after their evening out, they'd both been exhausted—by their day spent at the lagoon, and the brothel fantasy. They'd both fallen asleep the moment their heads hit their pillows, and they'd slept in later than they'd meant to this morning, which meant they had to rush to pack and eat a quick breakfast in order to get off the island on time.

Dean figured the best way to get inside Jillian's head and thoughts was to outright ask the question that was weighing heavily on his mind. She was gazing out the small window, and he placed his hand over hers on the armrest.

At this touch, she turned to face him, and smiled. There was no sign that she was troubled, but Dean had come a long way over the past few months in their relationship and knew just how important communication

THE CAPTURE

was in keeping his marriage strong and solid. Which meant if he had any concerns, he'd learned to air them so they didn't fester and cause bigger issues down the road.

"Are you okay?" he asked, needing to know.

She looked surprised by the question and tipped her head curiously. "Do I not seem okay to you?"

She seemed perfectly fine, but he realized he needed a verbal assurance that he hadn't pushed her too far. "We didn't talk much about last night and what happened at the brothel."

He'd definitely nudged her past her comfort zone in more than one way, and while she'd never used the safe word they'd established, he worried that she might harbor regrets after the fact. Having her submit to something that might be a hard limit for her would destroy him.

She was quiet for a moment, increasing that odd twist of uncertainty tangling up inside of him.

"Last night was . . . intense," she said thoughtfully, and when she glanced up and

ERIKA WILDE

saw the pained look on his face, she quickly sought to explain her comment. "Don't get me wrong, Dean. I loved what happened, along with everything else that transpired on Eden. I loved being captured and ravished by Black Heart," she added with a grin. "The entire weekend was hot and erotic and beyond my wildest imaginings, but I'm glad it was all a fantasy we can leave behind, because I love our reality even more."

He raised a brow as he threaded their fingers together, holding her hand in his. "Our reality?"

"You, and me, and living a normal life," she said, squeezing his hand affectionately. "You being my best friend, my husband, my amazing lover. I wouldn't trade any of those things for any fantasy in the world."

"Good to know." He agreed that fulfilling fantasies were fun and hot, but they didn't sustain a relationship or marriage. "Though just for the record, I'm having a great time indulging in *our* fantasies."

"Oh, me, too," she admitted, her eyes suddenly sparkling mischievously as she leaned in close to brush her lips against his

THE CAPTURE

ear. She placed a hand in his lap and trailed her fingers over the zipper of his jeans in a teasing caress. "In fact, about a week ago I pulled a fantasy you'd written out of our vase in the playroom, and I think right now is the perfect time to check it off both of our sexual bucket lists."

His randy cock stirred, hardening in anticipation, and he was grateful that they were alone and the pilot was otherwise occupied. "And which fantasy was that?"

She flashed him a seductive grin. "Why don't I show you."

Unbuckling her seatbelt, she knelt in front of his chair, opened the front of his jeans, and released his erection from the confines of his boxer-briefs. He exhaled a harsh breath when she stroked him in her hand, and groaned when she leaned forward and licked the head of his cock, then slid her hot, wet mouth down the length of him, until the crown bumped the back of her throat.

He tensed and hissed when she sucked her way back up, then dragged her teeth delicately over the swollen tip before swallowing him all over again. Her teasing eyes looked

ERIKA WILDE

up at him, and when he was good and hard and glistening wet, she finally stood up, lifted the skirt of her lightweight summer dress to her hips, and straddled his lap.

He caught a glimpse of her bare, waxed pussy, and realized that his wicked wife hadn't put any panties on this morning. She rubbed his cock all along her slick folds, positioned him, then slowly sank down on his straining, aching shaft. Her head dropped back on a shivery moan of pleasure, and then she began riding him, her hips sliding back and forth in a slow, leisurely pace.

Grabbing her waist, he matched her rhythm with his own deep thrusts.

She placed her hands on either side of his face, tipping his head back so their eyes met, and locked. "*This* fantasy," she murmured huskily, giving him a hot, deep, tongue-tangling kiss before whispering against his lips, "Welcome to the mile-high club, husband."


If you would like to know when my newest

book will be released, please sign up for my newsletter here: www.erikawilde.com/social-newsletter-sign-up

Other Books in
**The Marriage Diaries Series**
THE MARRIAGE DIARIES
THE INVITATION
THE CAPTURE

TO LEARN MORE about Erika Wilde and her upcoming releases, you can visit her at the following places on the web:

Website:

www.erikawilde.com

Facebook:

facebook.com/erikawildeauthorfanpage

Goodreads:

goodreads.com/erikawildeauthor

Made in the USA
Middletown, DE
07 March 2024